DATE DUE

The Place My
·W·O·R·D·S·
Are Looking For

What Poets Say About and
Through Their Work

Selected By

Paul B. Janeczko

Bradbury Press   New York

Bradbury Press
An Affiliate of Macmillan, Inc.
866 Third Avenue, New York, NY 10022
Collier Macmillan Canada, Inc.

Printed and bound in the United States of America

10 9 8 7 6 5 4 3

The text of this book is set in Usherwood Book and Gill Sans Light.
Book design by Molly Heron

LIBRARY OF CONGRESS CATALOGING-IN-PUBLICATION DATA

The Place my words are looking for : what poets say about and through their work / selected by Paul B. Janeczko.—1st ed.
p.   cm.
Summary: Thirty-nine United States poets share their poems, inspirations, thoughts, anecdotes, and memories.
ISBN 0-02-747671-5
1. Children's poetry, American.   2. Poetry—Authorship—Juvenile literature.   3. Poetry—Juvenile literature.   [1. American poetry—Collections.   2. Poets, American.   3. Poetry—Authorship.]
I. Janeczko, Paul B.
PS586.3.P5   1990
811.008'09282—dc20   89-39331   CIP   AC

For Luke Janeczko and Joshua Jezsik,
the new kids on the block,
with more than an uncle's love

CONTENTS

Part IV

The New Moon

EVE MERRIAM

Hold on to me.
We will slip carefully carefully
don't tip it over
into this canoe
pale as birch bark

and with the stars
over our shoulders
paddle
down the dark river
of the sky.

Do not delay.
By next week
the canoe will be bulging with cargo,
there will be no room
inside for us.

Tonight is the time.
Step carefully.
Hold on to me.

PART I

Esmé on Her Brother's Bicycle

RUSSELL HOBAN

One foot on, one foot pushing, Esmé starting
off beside
Wheels too tall to mount astride,
Swings the off leg forward featly,
Clears the high bar nimbly, neatly,
With a concentrated frown,
Bears the upper pedal down
As the lower rises, then
Brings her whole weight round again,
Leaning forward, gripping tight,
With her knuckles showing white,
Down the road goes, fast and small,
Never sitting down at all.

The Rider

NAOMI SHIHAB NYE

A boy told me
if he rollerskated fast enough
his loneliness couldn't catch up to him,

the best reason I ever heard
for trying to be a champion.

What I wonder tonight
pedaling hard down King William Street
is if it translates to bicycles.

A victory! To leave your loneliness
panting behind you on some street corner
while you float free into a cloud of sudden azaleas,
luminous pink petals that have never felt loneliness,
no matter how slowly they fell.

NAOMI SHIHAB NYE

o o o

For me poetry has always been a way of paying attention to the world. We hear so many voices every day, swirling around us, and a poem makes us slow down and listen carefully to a few things we have really heard, deep inside. For me poems usually begin with "true things"—people, experiences, quotes —but quickly ride off into that other territory of imagination, which lives alongside us as much as we will allow in a world that likes to pay too much attention to "facts" sometimes. I have always had a slight difficulty distinguishing where the "true" part ends and the "made-up" part begins, because I think of dreaming and imagining as being another kind of *true*. Once I made up a song that ends, "You tell me what's real, what I see or what I feel?", and I think that corresponds to the poems we make out of our lives.

Sometimes there's no one to listen to what you really might like to say at a certain moment. The paper will always listen. Also, the more you write, the paper will begin to speak back and allow you to discover new parts of your own life and other lives and feel how things connect. Poets are explorers, pilgrims. Most of the poets I know are not in the least bit frilly. Poets are also regular people who live down the block and do simple things like wash clothes and stir soup. Sometimes students ask, "Are you famous?", as if fame is what would make a poet happy. I prefer the idea of being invisible, traveling through the world lightly, seeing and remembering as much as I can.

N. S. N.

The Sidewalk Racer
OR

On the Skateboard

LILLIAN MORRISON

Skimming
an asphalt sea
I swerve, I curve, I
sway; I speed to whirring
sound an inch above the
ground; I'm the sailor
and the sail, I'm the
driver and the wheel
I'm the one and only
single engine
human auto
mobile.

LILLIAN MORRISON

o o o

Skateboards were not around when I was growing up but I roller-skated and rode scooters with fierce enjoyment, and in writing "The Sidewalk Racer" I imagined the possible feelings of the skateboarders I like to watch on my street. The words and images for this poem just came. It has plenty of rhymes and rhythm, but the rhymes are not at the end of each line because, just for fun, I put the poem in the form of a skateboard. Words, word sounds, and rhythms excite me. I have always loved sports and dance, so my poems often deal with motion or have a strong feeling of body movement in them. When you read a poem, you get more out of it if you read it aloud or hear the words in your head and sense the rhythms along with the meanings as you read silently.

Writing poems can be a way of pinning down a dream (almost); capturing a moment, a memory, a happening; and, at the same time, it's a way of sorting out your thoughts and feelings. Sometimes the words tell you what you didn't know you knew.

L. M.

At the Playground

WILLIAM STAFFORD

Away down deep and away up high,
a swing drops you into the sky.
Back, it draws you away down deep,
forth, it flings you in a sweep
all the way to the stars and back
—Goodby, Jill; Goodby, Jack:
shuddering climb wild and steep,
away up high, away down deep.

• • •

Mosquito

J. PATRICK LEWIS

I was climbing up the sliding board
When suddenly I felt
A Mosquito bite my bottom
And it raised a big red welt.
So I said to that Mosquito,
"I'm sure you wouldn't mind
If I took a pair of tweezers
And I tweezered *your* behind?"

He shriveled up his body,
He shuffled to his feet.
He said, "I'm awfully sorry
But a fellow's got to eat!
There *are* Mosquito manners!
And I must have just forgot 'em.
I swear I'll never never NEVER
Bite another bottom."

But a minute later Archie Hill
And Buck and Theo Brown
Were horsing on the monkey bars,
Hanging upside down.
They must have looked delicious
From a skeeter's point of view
'Cause he bit 'em on the bottoms—
Archie, Buck and Theo, too!

You could hear 'em going HOLY–!
  You could hear 'em going WHACK!
    You could hear 'em cuss and holler,
      Going SMACK—SMACK—SMACK!

A Mosquito's awful sneaky,
A Mosquito's mighty sly,
But I never never NEVER
Thought a skeeter'd tell a lie!

J. PATRICK LEWIS

o o o

One thing that has fascinated me from childhood on—through *The Wind in the Willows, Alice in Wonderland,* the great classics —is the magic of animals doing the talking. So instead of trying consciously to discover what appeals to a third grader's mysterious mind, I'm more likely to write a poem as seen through the eyes of a giraffe, a crocodile, maybe even a blue-footed booby.

In these strange and serious times, I want to try a little silliness—wordplay or nonsense verse—where, for instance, a mosquito can explain what mosquitoes do best.

J.P.L.

I Can't Go Back to School

MICHAEL PATRICK HEARN

The cat! The cat!
She ate my hat!
I don't know where my shirt is!
Just look at this sweater!
I wish it looked better!
Just look how thick the dirt is!
How can I dress?
My hair's a mess!
I look just like a fool!
I can't go back to school like this!
I can't go back to school!

MICHAEL PATRICK HEARN

o o o

Where do poems come from? Out of thin air? I never really know where. But what usually happens is someone calls me up and asks, "Do you have a witch poem?" Or, "I need one about giants." Or, "Got something about going back to school?" Or, "How about a winter poem?" And I always answer, "Sure." Then I think and I worry and I think and I go to bed. (I do my best writing in my sleep.) It usually comes to me in the middle of the night. I draw from all sorts of verse—jingles, folk songs, rock songs, opera, jazz.... But I learn the most from listening to others just talking. I become a tall, skinny, curly-haired, pale-faced, short-tempered kid. His is the voice I use. I always liked nonsense verse and story poems. I always liked bright wordplay and marvelous imagery. I did not like lyric verse. Poetry was always a wonderful game, the magical juggling of rhythm and rhyme and sense and sound. Sometimes I hit the mark, sometimes not.

I write what I would have liked to have read when I was nine years old. And what I would not be ashamed of reading now.

M. P. H.

The Underwater Wibbles

JACK PRELUTSKY

The Underwater Wibbles
dine exclusively on cheese,
they keep it in containers
which they bind about their knees,
they often chew on Cheddar
which they slice into a dish,
and gorge on Gorgonzola
to the wonder of the fish.

The Underwater Wibbles
wiggle blithely through the sea,
munching merrily on Muenster,
grated Feta, bits of Brie,
passing porpoises seem puzzled,
stolid octopuses stare,
as the Wibbles nibble Gouda,
Provolone, Camembert.

The Underwater Wibbles
frolic gaily off the coast,
eating melted Mozzarella
served on soggy crusts of toast,
Wibbles gobble Appenzeller
as they execute their dives,
oh, the Underwater Wibbles
live extraordinary lives.

© 1986 Jonathan A. Meyers

JACK PRELUTSKY

o o o

"The Underwater Wibbles" is an odd poem, even for me. I distinctly recall writing it in the bathtub. That in itself isn't unusual, for I've gotten quite a few ideas in the tub, but it's one of the few times when the medium became the message. I was taking a long soak and had a variety of snacks close at hand, notably an assortment of cheeses. Inspiration can strike unexpectedly —when I carelessly dropped a small wedge of Camembert, a poem was born. As I fished about for the submerged morsel, I did some free-associating and came up with the notion of bizarre underwater creatures who live on a strict cheese diet. The rest was a lot of fun and a little work. I scribbled out a few notes on waterproof paper with my underwater pen, both of which I keep handy for these occasions. Later, when I was dry and back in my studio, I began to build the poem, listing an exotic array of cheeses. I included hard varieties, soft and cream types, and at least one with visible mold. I also took some pains to pay homage to the major cheese-producing nations.

About twenty years earlier, I had written a short and undistinguished verse about a rubbery creature that I called the Wibble. I took the liberty of borrowing from myself, and "The Underwater Wibbles" was soon a "feta acccompli."

J. P.

We Heard Wally Wail

JACK PRELUTSKY

We heard Wally wail through the whole
    neighborhood,
as his mother whaled Wally as hard as she could,
she made Wally holler, she made Wally whoop,
for what he had spelled in the alphabet soup.

• • •

There Was a Man

PHYLLIS JANOWITZ

My neighbor has a wooden leg
               (thump, thump)
he drags on the ground.
He tells children to bang on it.

They're afraid they'll hurt him
and bang very gently
               (tap, tap)
He takes out his teeth

To show them
what a fake he is.
They are amazed!

He takes off his glasses
like the man who
scratched his eyes
out and in again.

Then he hides pennies
for them to find and keep.
Finally he takes off his wooden leg
               (thump, thump)
and leans it against the wall.

Photo by Hank De Leo

PHYLLIS JANOWITZ

o o o

When I was five years old, my Uncle Leo (who died many years ago) told me that he was a very special person for a number of reasons: He could take off his eyes (eyeglasses) and put them back on, he could take out his teeth and put them back in, and he could take off his leg (a wooden one). Then, at other times, he'd say, "I'm so strong if you hit my leg it won't even hurt. Go on, hit me, hit me!" I wouldn't want to hit him, even if it didn't hurt; I loved him very much. He was a magician. He could turn a handkerchief into a mouse and make it jump out of his hand. And he would hide pennies in the living room for my sister and me to find. He had a huge crop of white hair, carried a cane, and looked fierce. Men don't look like this anymore—elegant and strong. I, for one, don't ever see any quite as handsome.

P.J.

When My Friends
All Moved Away

STEVEN KROLL

When my friends all moved away
I thought I wouldn't last a day.

Now I visit them by bus
And wonder why I made a fuss.

Photo by Henry Bolan

STEVEN KROLL

o   o   o

I am not a poet. I am a writer who sometimes writes poetry. This may mean that I don't take the writing of poetry as seriously as some poets do, but then, I suppose, it becomes fair to question the real meaning of seriousness.

Most of the poems I write are funny, or at least I hope they are. Humor, of course, has its own kind of seriousness, but I think my poems come out funny—people like to call them "nonsense poems"—because of my exuberant response to the world.

For me, ideas turn into poems rather than stories when the energy behind them cannot be contained by the prose form. My poems are written in bouncy, antic rhyme or, frequently, eccentric meter. They are sometimes silly, sometimes totally bizarre. They tend to come in a rush, to be fully formed and finished almost before I can write them down, to appear in my head in rows, the way Stephen Crane said his did.

I enjoy writing poems so much, I should probably write more of them than I do.

S. K.

74th Street

MYRA COHN LIVINGSTON

Hey, this little kid gets roller skates.
She puts them on.
She stands up and almost
flops over backwards.
She sticks out a foot like
she's going somewhere and
falls down and
smacks her hand. She
grabs hold of a step to get up and
sticks out the other foot and
slides about six inches and
falls and
skins her knee.

And then, you know what?

She brushes off the dirt and the
blood and puts some
spit on it and then
sticks out the other foot

again.

We Could Be Friends

MYRA COHN LIVINGSTON

We could be friends
Like friends are supposed to be.
You, picking up the telephone
Calling me

    to come over and play
    or take a walk,
    finding a place
    to sit and talk,

Or just goof around
Like friends do,
Me, picking up the telephone
Calling you.

© Marilyn Sanders 1986

MYRA COHN LIVINGSTON

o   o   o

Loneliness, a search for friends, alienation from others have always concerned me. Again and again, sharing poetry or teaching children something about the craft of poetry, I am struck by the inability of so many to know how to approach another human being, to even admit to a loneliness which, if truth be told, every one of us feels at times. How do we deal with this inability to know what to say, to reach out for friendship, to find the common ground on which we might walk together?

In "We Could Be Friends" I am suggesting that passivity—waiting for another to take the first step, make the initial gesture—is not always the way. It is not "you picking up the telephone calling me" but "me picking up the telephone calling you" that may lead to friendship.

An ideal friendship is, of course, a give-and-take relationship, with both friends initiating as well as receiving calls. So the poem, I believe, also works for those who are not searching but have already found friendship.

M. C. L.

The Paragon

BOBBI KATZ

Yuk! How I hate Nancy Feder!
I can't think why the world would need her.
Since Nancy Feder moved next door,
life's not worth living anymore.
I don't know how my mother knows
she makes her bed and folds her clothes
and does her homework everyday
before she goes outside to play.
She's such a goodie, goodie, good—
she'd make you barf! I bet she would!
(And you don't have to listen to
my mother rave the way I do!)
A rabbit's foot might bring me luck,
and then I'll see a moving truck.
Won't it be a sunny day,
when Nancy Feder moves away?

BOBBI KATZ

o o o

I write poetry for the same reason I read it: the sound of words, their taste on my tongue, is irresistible. Words are the apple pie in my pantry that draws me out of my warm bed and sends me shuffling down the dark cold hall in the middle of the night!

Poetry lets me do all the things I can't do in other media: paint a picture, sing a song, capture a moment on film, express an emotion without using "psycho-speak" (my name for all those modish clichés). And best of all, when I write rhyming poems I can even play decent tennis—joyfully volleying the ball over the net and returning it with the next line!

Rhyme seems to automatically quicken and lighten a poem, regardless of the subject. Sometimes I can't make rhyme convey my feelings. I wish I could!

On the other hand, free verse is infinitely more difficult for me. Without the boundaries of a rhyme scheme and fixed meter, I find it harder to say what I want with economy. Writing free verse is my chance to join the circus! I walk across a tightrope, high off the ground. Carefully I put one foot in front of the other—completely absorbed by the going, never quite knowing where the rope will end.

B. K.

The Games of Night

NANCY WILLARD

The ghost comes. I don't see her.
I smell the licorice drops in her pocket.
I climb out of bed, I draw her bath.
She has come a long way, and I know she's tired.

By the light of the moon, the water splashes.
By the light of the stars, the soap leaps,
it dives, it pummels the air,
it scrubs off the dust of not-seeing,

and I see her sandals, black like mine
and I see her dress, white like mine.
Little by little, she comes clear.
She rises up in a skin of water.

As long as the water shines, I can see her.
As long as I see her, we can play
by the light of the moon on my bed,
by the light of the stars on my bear
till the sun opens its eye, the sun that wakes things,
the sun that doesn't believe in ghosts.

Photo by Eric Lindbloom

NANCY WILLARD

○ ○ ○

I think the best way to enjoy poetry is to read it out loud. When I'm cleaning the house, I like to hear poetry, on tape or on a record. Poems were around long before books. They came to our ancestors through hearing them rather than reading them.

I once had a teacher who made his students memorize poems. On Fridays we had to write out in class the poems we'd learned by heart. Of course we grumbled about it. But now those poems come back to me when I need them. The full moon looks in at me, and I greet her with lines from a poem by Emily Dickinson.

> The moon was but a chin of gold
> A night or two ago,
> And now she turns her perfect face
> Upon the world below.

And what a privilege to be
But the remotest star!
For certainly her way might pass
Beside your twinkling door.

That's what it means to know a poem by heart. It's a gift from someone who feels the way you do, it doesn't wear out, and you can enjoy it over and over again.

N. W.

Pet Rock

CYNTHIA RYLANT

Roger came to Beaver
and fell in love
with me.
Big gorilla boy
with long arms
and a confused look.
Proved his devotion
by sitting on the couch
for *hours*
reading all my comics.

After a while
I learned to accept him
like a piece of furniture.
And lived my life
as if he weren't there.
Occasionally offered him
food and drink,
unsure how long love
could sustain him.
And when Pet Rocks became popular,
decided I didn't
need one, really,
having Roger.

KARLA KUSKIN

I have a friend who keeps on standing on her hands.
That's fine,
Except I find it very difficult to talk to her
Unless I stand on mine.

What We Might Be,
What We Are

X. J. KENNEDY

If you were a scoop of vanilla
And I were the cone where you sat,
If you were a slowly pitched baseball
And I were the swing of a bat,

If you were a shiny new fishhook
And I were a bucket of worms,
If we were a pin and a pincushion,
We might be on intimate terms.

If you were a plate of spaghetti
And I were your piping-hot sauce,
We'd not even need to write letters
To put our affection across.

But you're just a piece of red ribbon
In the beard of a Balinese goat
And I'm a New Jersey mosquito.
I guess we'll stay slightly remote.

X. J. KENNEDY

o o o

Kids often ask me, "Where do you get your ideas?"—a good question, but one that assumes that a poem always starts from an idea. With me that is seldom the case. A poem is most likely to arise when I haven't an idea in the world. It usually begins with a promising blob of language.

Sometimes, when I wake up early in the morning, a poem will start waking up, too. That's a fruitful time, that half hour in bed when I haven't yet shaken off dreams. A line of verse will come swimming lazily into mind, like a trout defiantly frisking its tail at a fisherman. I know that it's verse, for it has a bouncy beat to it. If I'm lucky, a second line will occur—maybe a line that rhymes with the first. These lines, by the way, aren't always the opening of a poem. They might be an ending, a middle, or anything.

A nice thing about writing in rhyme is that you don't need ideas to get you going. In fact, if you set out with a fixed idea in mind, rhymes will do their best to divert you from it. You intend to write a poem about dogs, say, and *poodle* is the first word you're going to find a rhyme for. You might want to talk about police dogs, Saint Bernards, and terriers, but your need for a rhyme will lead you to *noodle* and *strudel*. The darned poem will make you forget about dogs and write about food instead.

So I figure I might as well just fool around with words and let an idea happen. The tremendous fun of writing in rhyme is reeling in whatever it is you've caught and being surprised by it. If you're lucky, you just keep landing one line after another, like a fisherman stacking up his limit. When things go swimmingly, a sleek idea will come thrashing up to the surface right there and then, while you write.

X. J. K.

• • •

The Panteater

WILLIAM COLE

The Panteater
Looks something like an Anteater,
But his diet is more peculiar.
(I wouldn't fool ya.)
He doesn't eat ants,
Oh, no, no. He eats *pants!*
but worse than that—oh, wow!
Is that he only eats one trou!
The Panteater doesn't care if they're dress pants,
    slacks, or jeans,
He scarfs down half-pants like you gobble pork
    and beans.
So watch out—if you have a pair of trousers
    hanging on the line,
The Panteater might wander by to dine.
(And I know that you would never want to have
    it get about
That you'd been seen around the town with one
    knee hanging out.)

WILLIAM COLE

o   o   o

I suppose I could say that what I do in verse is find a good idea and rhyme it up. Take "The Panteater." Once I had the idea of the creature, it followed to describe what it looked like and then what it does.

I'm pretty severe with myself when it comes to rhyme and meter; my poems must have both. Oddly, I know nothing about poetic form; I don't know a sestina from a triolet, iambic from trochaic. I just do it. Oh yes, I recognize a limerick when I see one. In fact, I *dislike* a limerick when I see one—they're too easy.

Why do I write poems? Because it's fun: writing a poem for kids is something like working out a puzzle, testing my wit. And because I love poetry of any kind. I've been reading poetry all my life, since as a boy I discovered the pleasures of, say, the *Rubaiyat of Omar Khayyam*, or the simple poems of Longfellow. Then I followed the normal progression of any poetry lover: the playful joy of E.E. Cummings; the heavier stuff of Shakespeare, Yeats, Eliot, Auden; and on to my contemporaries, Philip Larkin and Seamus Heaney.

W. Somerset Maugham, a disagreeable man from all reports, wrote novels, plays, criticism, and no poetry. But he's quoted as saying, "The crown of literature is poetry. It is its end and aim. It is the sublimest activity of the human mind. It is the achievement of beauty and delicacy. The writer of prose can only step aside when the poet passes."

W. C.

• • •

A Story That Could Be True

WILLIAM STAFFORD

If you were exchanged in the cradle and
your real mother died
without ever telling the story
then no one knows your name,
and somewhere in the world
your father is lost and needs you
but you are far away.

He can never find
how true you are, how ready.
When the great wind comes
and the robberies of the rain
you stand on the corner shivering.
The people who go by—
you wonder at their calm.

They miss the whisper that runs
any day in your mind,
"Who are you really, wanderer?"
and the answer you have to give
no matter how dark and cold
the world around you is:
"Maybe I'm a king."

Suppose

SIV CEDERING

Suppose I were as clever as a bird
and the words for what I am
could be contained
in one precise song,
repeated, repeated
while each jubilant phrase
spells it all
in variations
too refined for the human ear

Or that the song has not yet been found
but waits inside me
like the long note that sounds
when a blade of grass
is placed between the thumbs
and blown

It could be
that the place my words are looking for
will turn out to be so small
that there will be room for nothing
but silence
—or an ocean so large
some waves will never reach
the sound of the shore

Speech Class
(for Joe)

JIM DANIELS

We were outcasts—
you with your stutters,
me with my slurring—
and that was plenty for a friendship.

When we left class to go to the therapist
we hoped they wouldn't laugh—
took turns reminding the teacher:
"Me and Joe have to go to shpeesh clash now,"
or "M-m-me and J-Jim ha-have to go to
    s-s-speech now."

Mrs. Clark, therapist, was also god, friend, mother.
Once she took us to the zoo on a field trip:
"Aw, ya gonna go look at the monkeys?"
"Maybe they'll teach you how to talk."
We clenched teeth and went
and felt the sun and fed the animals
and we were a family of broken words.

For years we both tried so hard
and I finally learned
where to put my tongue and how to make the sounds
and graduated,

but the first time you left class without me
I felt that punch in the gut—
I felt like a deserter
and wanted you
to have my voice.

JIM DANIELS

o o o

It's hard to say exactly why I write poetry—I've given different answers on different occasions—but maybe it's connected to how I first began to write back when I was in grade school.

I went to remedial speech class from kindergarten to eighth grade. I had problems with s, *sh*, *j*, *z*, *ch*. Especially *s*. If another kid wanted to get me mad, all he had to do was make fun of the way I talked. I got in a lot of fights because the only way I could defend myself was to rush at the kid making fun of me. Once he made fun of my speech, I was rendered speechless. If I said anything, it would be calling more attention to my defect.

I ended up being a pretty quiet kid. I used to lie in bed at night practicing my speech sounds after I said my prayers. While I practiced my sounds, I thought about what had happened that

45

day. Often, I wished I'd said or done something that I had held inside. I shared a room with my younger brother, and it was years later that he told me he'd thought those sounds were a part of some strange prayer only I had to say. And I realize now that they were a kind of prayer—the sound exercises were like a religious chant that freed my mind to let in the stray subconscious thought. At some point, I began to write down those thoughts.

I often think that I started writing poetry at such an early age because of my speech defect, but I probably would have come to it eventually, speech defect or no, because I became addicted to the freedom of the page, to saying whatever I wanted without having to think about what other people thought. Eventually, I did have to be concerned with that, but early on, it was just me and the paper, the paper that didn't make fun of what I said or how I said it.

J.D.

What I Remember About the 6th Grade

MARK VINZ

We lost the school softball championship
when that four-eyed kid popped out
with the bases loaded. We did win the
spelling bee, though. Weird Charlie said
it was because we had the ugliest girls.

The Scarlet Tanager edged out the Wood Duck
in our balloting for the State Bird
because the girls liked red and organized.
I voted for the Bluejay or maybe the Loon.
Weird Charlie voted for the Crow.

The teacher nearly got knocked cold when
a big picture of George Washington or somebody
fell off the wall and conked her on the head.
Most of the girls cried. Most of the boys
laughed, especially Weird Charlie.

Once a month or so they'd herd us
to the basement for atomic bomb drills
and films of houses exploding in firestorms.
When it came to the Nuclear Age,
even Weird Charlie kept his mouth shut.

PART II

Puzzled

MARGARET HILLERT

I took a sip of lemon pop
And then a sip of lime,
A little orange soda, too,
A swallow at a time.
Some grape came next and cherry red,
And then I almost cried.
How *could* my stomach feel so bad
With rainbows down inside?

MARGARET HILLERT

o   o   o

I'm often asked, "Do you like to write poetry?" and "Is it fun?"
To the first I can only respond that whether I like to write it or
not, I *have* to write it. If I get an idea I am compelled to work
it out. I have had such feelings ever since writing my first poem
in the third grade.

As for whether it is "fun," I would say it is, in a way, but it is
also a lot of hard work. A poem doesn't usually come to me
whole, but if I have the inkling of an idea I try to work it through,
and this can take days or years. Even then some things continue
to be only scraps in a notebook and never get finished.

For me a poem doesn't always start at the beginning. The
idea may be a word, a phrase, or a whole sentence that eventually turns up anywhere in the poem, depending on what I do
with it and how much I revise to say exactly what I want to say.
Since there is no new subject matter I try to treat ideas in fresh,

original ways. I like to work with rather traditional forms, but the fun comes in the playing with words and the sounds of words; in the use of varied rhythms and rhyme schemes; in the musicality of rhyme, alliteration, and other poetic devices.

Of course, if the poem should happen to be published it is certainly "fun" to see my name in print.

M. H.

A Hot Property

RONALD WALLACE

I am not. I am
an also-ran,
a bridesmaid, a finalist,
a second-best bed. I am
the one they could just
as easily have given it to
but didn't.
I'm a near miss, a close second,
an understudy, a runner-up.
I'm the one who was just
edged, shaded, bested, nosed out.
I made the final cut,
the short list,
the long deliberation.
I'm good, very good,
but I'm not good enough.
I'm an alternate, a backup,
a very close decision,
a red ribbon, a handshake,
a glowing commendation.
You don't know me.
I've a dozen names,
all honorably mentioned.
I could be anybody.

RONALD WALLACE

o o o

It is the fall of seventh grade, a muggy, hot, St. Louis afternoon.
I'm sitting at my desk in the back corner of old Mrs. Alison's
English class, the last class of the day. Mrs. Alison is handing out
some faded mimeograph sheets for twenty minutes of silent
reading. Earlier in the period Bob Castleburg pulled the plastic
vomit trick, placing the novelty beside his desk, covering his
mouth, and asking to be excused. Mrs. Alison lectured us about
laughing at other people's misfortune, and called in Mr. Orton,
the janitor, who, seeing the joke for what it was, sprinkled
sawdust on the "vomit" and swept it into his pan. Now, unnerved
by the class and wearied by the heat, Mrs. Alison resorts once
again to mimeograph sheets.

They are Emily Dickinson poems. I have never read Emily
Dickinson before, and as I begin to read, something curious

happens. The class and its laughter fade, Bob Castleburg fades, even Mrs. Alison, her head thudding heavily on her desk as she leans into sleep, fades, and I'm left in the presence of the rare and strange, feeling (as I would later learn Emily Dickinson herself put it) as if the top of my head were taken off. I don't understand the poems, but I feel their power—their terror and joy and exhilaration and surprise and whimsy—and when the bell rings I don't hear it. Neither does Mrs. Alison.

Thirty years pass, faster than I could have imagined. I know a lot about Emily Dickinson now—how she wrote her poems on slips of paper and showed them to few people in her lifetime (1830–1886); how early editors rewrote her poems to make them less strange for readers, and how the poems weren't published as *she* wrote them until 1955; how she is now considered to be one of America's greatest poets; how deeply she has influenced my own work. And I know that if I have a goal as a poet, it is to do for a reader what Emily Dickinson did for me: to write poems that will surprise, delight, tease, move, and terrify—poems that will keep you reading right through the bell.

R. W.

Famous

NAOMI SHIHAB NYE

The river is famous to the fish.

The loud voice is famous to silence,
which knew it would inherit the earth
before anybody said so.

The cat sleeping on the fence is famous to the birds
watching him from the birdhouse.

The tear is famous, briefly, to the cheek.

The idea you carry close to your bosom
is famous to your bosom.

The boot is famous to the earth,
more famous than the dress shoe,
which is famous only to floors.

The bent photograph is famous to the one who
    carries it
and not at all famous to the one who is pictured.

I want to be famous to shuffling men
who smile while crossing streets,
sticky children in grocery lines,
famous as the one who smiled back.

I want to be famous in the way a pulley is famous,
or a buttonhole, not because it did anything
    spectacular,
but because it never forgot what it could do.

One Time

WILLIAM STAFFORD

When evening had flowed between houses
and paused on the schoolground, I met
Hilary's blind little sister following
the gray smooth railing still warm from the sun
with her hand; and she stood by the edge
holding her face upward waiting
while the last light found her cheek
and her hair, and then on over the trees.

You could hear the great sprinkler arm
of water find and then leave the pavement,
and pigeons telling each other their dreams
or the dreams they would have. We were
deep in the well of shadow by then, and I
held out my hand, saying, "Tina, it's me—
Hilary says I should tell you it's dark,
and, oh, Tina, it is. Together now—"

And I reached, our hands touched,
and we found our way home.

Photo by Kit Stafford

WILLIAM STAFFORD

o   o   o

Talk with a little luck in it, that's what poetry is—just let the words take you where *they* want to go. You'll be invited; things will happen; your life will have more in it than other people's lives have.

Of course this kind of luck happens to everybody, when they get going in their talk or in their writing, but only those who pay attention and try in a sustained way get richer and richer in their lives.

Once someone said to me, "Think of something that happened, but don't tell what happened—tell what you wish had happened. And try to remember more of your feelings than just the look of things; tell how they felt, how they sounded, whatever. . . ." That's how my poem "One Time" came to me. I began to feel how the sun warmed the railing by the school. I could hear the pigeons "telling their dreams." And with a great rush I felt how it would be to be blind, to have the world out there signaling to you all the time.

W. S.

A Little Girl's Poem

GWENDOLYN BROOKS

Life is for me and is shining!
Inside me I
feel stars and sun and bells singing.

There are children in the world
all around me and beyond me—
here, and beyond the big waters;
here, and in countries peculiar to me
but not peculiar to themselves.

I want the children to live and to laugh.
I want them to sit with their mothers
    and fathers
and have happy cocoa together.

I do not want
fire screaming up to the sky.
I do not want
families killed in their doorways.

Life is for us, for the children.
Life is for mothers and fathers,
life is for the tall girls and boys
in the high school on Henderson Street,
is for the people in Afrikan tents,

the people in English cathedrals,
the people in Indian courtyards;
the people in cottages all over the world.

Life is for us, and is shining.
We have a right to sing.

GWENDOLYN BROOKS

o o o

In your poems, talk about what you know. Talk about what you think. Talk about what you feel. Talk about what you wonder.

COLLECT WORDS!

Buy your *own* dictionary. Read your dictionary every day. CIRCLE exciting words. The more words you know, the *better* you will be able to express yourself, your thoughts.

Be yourself. Do not imitate other poets. You are as important as they are.

Do not be afraid to say something NEW.

In *some* of your poems, BE A LITTLE MYSTERIOUS! Surprise yourself and your reader!

G. B.

Computer

GWENDOLYN BROOKS

A computer is a machine.
A machine is interesting.
A machine is useful.
I can study a computer.
I can use it.

Who made it?
Human beings made it.

I am a human being.
I am warm. I am wise.
I have empathies for animals and
    people.

I conduct a computer.
A computer does not conduct me.

• • •

New Love

EVE MERRIAM

I am telling my hands
not to blossom into roses

I am telling my feet
not to turn into birds
and fly over rooftops

and I am putting a hat on my head
so the flaming meteors
in my hair
will hardly show.

EVE MERRIAM

o o o

Writing poetry is where my heart is. Growing up in Phila-delphia, my brother and I were taken to Gilbert and Sullivan, and we used to chant all those tongue-twisting verses of Gilbert's. The local column of the *Philadelphia Bulletin* printed light verse, and my brother and I would read aloud, declaiming, "I eat my peas with honey,/ I have done it all my life./ They do taste kind of funny,/ But it keeps them on the knife." I devoured poetry of all kinds—narrative, dramatic, limericks, whatever, and I would never beware of the doggerel.

Sounds of words were enthralling: I was captivated by their musicality, and by the fact that you could have alliteration, so that if you said, "Peter, Peter, Pumpkin Eater," it was very funny. Or if you recited "The Highway Man came riding, riding, up to the old inn door," it was exciting; you could hear a whole or-chestra in your voice.

I started writing verses when I was quite young, and by the time I got into high school I was writing serious poems for the school magazine, as well as political and light verse for the weekly newspaper at school. It never occurred to me that someday I would like to be a writer. I simply wrote. I think one is chosen to be a poet; you write poems because you must, because you cannot live your life without writing them.

Sometimes I've spent weeks looking for precisely the right word. It's like having a tiny marble in your pocket; you can feel it. Sometimes you find a word and say, "No, I don't think this is precisely it...." Then you discard it, and take another and another until you get it right. What I'd like to stress above everything else is the joy of the sounds of language. I have only one rule for reading it: please read a poem OUT LOUD.

E. M.

Late

NAOMI SHIHAB NYE

Your street was named for berries
so we dug and dug in heaps of leaves.
The door to your basement
would never stay closed.
Uncle said to push it till it clicked.
"Come eat!" you'd call,
planting yourself by the table.
We came in with twigs in our hair.

At the bottom of those stairs
was a tomb where old sofas went
and milk bottles grew spider nests.
We stayed outside till the light shrank
into its last deep moment of staring
and the moon came up like a giant other eye.

One night we fooled you,
hiding under the bush,
the yard was a held breath.
Your voice trilled for us,
rose higher on its ladder
till it was not calling for us at all,
it was reaching for everything you dreamed of
that never happened,
the years flying out of your skin,
the shadowy baby who wouldn't be born.

We came in sheepishly, looking at our feet.
Today I would answer for all those other things.

Circles

MYRA COHN LIVINGSTON

I am speaking of circles.

The circle we made around the table,
our hands brushing as we passed potatoes.
The circle we made in our potatoes
to pour in gravy, whorling in its round bowl.
The circle we made every evening
finding our own place at the table
with its own napkin in its own ring.

I am speaking of circles broken.

Enchantment

JOANNE RYDER

On warm summer nights
the porch becomes our living room
where Mama takes her reading
and Dad and I play games
in the patch of brightness
the lamp scatters on the floor.
From the darkness, others come—
small round bodies
clinging to the screens
which separate us
from the yard beyond.
Drawn to our light,
the June bugs watch our games
and listen to our talk till bedtime
when Mama darkens the porch
and breaks the spell
that holds them close to us.

Yellow Sonnet

PAUL ZIMMER

Zimmer no longer wishes to write
About the dimming of his lights,
Recounting all his small terrors.
Instead he tells of brilliance,
Walking home from first grade
In springtime, light descending
To hold itself and dazzle him
In an outburst of dandelions.
It was then he learned that
He would always love yellow,
Its warm dust on his knuckles,
The memory of gathering pieces
To carry home in his lunch pail
As a love gift for his mother.

PAUL ZIMMER

o o o

Regarding "Yellow Sonnet," my mother had died about a year before I wrote this. She was eighty-two and had been sick and uncomfortable for a while, so she was ready when the time came. But I miss her very much. One of the things a poet can do with his work is remember people and very special times. When she died I felt very dismal. It made me sense my own mortality. I wrote some sad poems.

But my mother had been very good to me and I have many warm and bright memories of her. I wanted to make a warm and bright poem in her memory, something that was worthy of her. One of my favorite colors is yellow. I have sometimes wondered why. Then I remembered the instance of discovering the dandelions when I was a very small child. The poem gave me an opportunity to present a loving tribute to my mother. I worked hard on it and it became a sonnet. I am very grateful for it. I believe she would have liked it. I would have given it to her as I gave her the dandelions as a child. It is a love gift. It has helped me to bear my loss.

P. Z.

Forgotten

CYNTHIA RYLANT

Mom came home one day
and said my father had died.
Her eyes all red.
Crying for some stranger.
Couldn't think of anything to do,
so I walked around Beaver
telling the kids
and feeling important.
Nobody else's dad had died.
But then
nobody else's dad had worn
red-striped pajamas
and nobody else's dad had made
stuffed animals talk
and nobody else's dad had gone away
nine years ago.
Nobody else's dad had been so loved
by a four-year-old.
And so forgotten by one
now
thirteen.

Carousel

JULIA CUNNINGHAM

That calliope really cancelled me out
I mean I couldn't joggle myself together again
what with the notes burbling and bumping and bashing
and my heart responding in irregular beats.
What was it? What voices hid inside that turning
of horses and swans and dragons?
Why were they calling me back
dragging my spirit by the heels
until I was nine again?
He stood there, waving, my lost father
with no more love to catch me
than then.

JULIA CUNNINGHAM

o o o

Poetry is, to me, a place to be. I first discovered these places—they are many—at the age of about twelve. The journeys to these refuges from hurt, sadness, puzzlement, and misunderstandings turned into poems that healed and helped and made of me a very grateful writer. Poems also of delight and joy, of ventures to mountains, beech groves, meadows, and the shores of the sea gave me freedom only the traveller into the imagination can know.

And now, many years from twelve, I can only ask that you, too, all of you, walk with your words into these secret, mysterious, and magic places where poems lead you.

J. C.

A short long story

JULIA CUNNINGHAM

They mocked him when he said
he met a bear on the beach
a bear with wings
and even though he was not quite old enough
being seven, to be called a liar
it was:
Oh, don't be silly
He really should get over such nonsense
He needs a firm hand
School, school will get it out of him
and even through all this he stood up
and repeated:
I did, I saw a small, brown bear
with wings the color of my mother's eyes.
This mention of the mother
halted the others
for she'd only been dead a year
and maybe the boy still missed her
making him foolish.
When he said it again
his father left his martini
took his hand and went with him
back to the sea, out of sight,

When they returned his father spoke, quietly,
I saw the bear
He saw the wings
and the boy smiled.

Humming Bird

FELICE HOLMAN

Whirring as wound wires whir.
Glistened green and brightened blur.
Bird a flower dreamed upon.
A moment fanning, and then gone.

FELICE HOLMAN

o o o

Poetry came into my life early, just as it does for most children. It was just part of being, like eating, sleeping, playing. It was *there* singing all around. I suppose first it was nursery rhymes, then *A Child's Garden of Verses* (I still have my own old, shredded, loved-to-death volume). After that there was just a real Fourth of July explosion of wonderful poets beating rhythms and rhymes that fascinated me.

As soon as I could write, I wrote poetry, and I guess I must have got stuck then because I'm still doing it. Why? Because it is *so* satisfying. A thought springs to one's mind from the ether, then turns to words that fall into lines and shapes and sounds, get rearranged, form a picture, shout a feeling, weep, laugh. . . . And all in time to see the whole thing come to fruition, hold the finished work in one's hand, sometimes without even missing dinner.

There is something about poems that is like loving children: They keep returning home and singing to you all your life.

F. H.

White on White

CHRISTINE E. HEMP

Today my father is painting
everything white for the wedding.
He's painting the porch, the bench,
the window sash for my sister;
he's slapping a coat on the flagpole too.

I asked him if he was painting
the steps and he said, "everything
already white I am painting."
I wonder if the baby's breath, the
daisies, or even the cat will be

daubed with creamy sploshes.
Or maybe the clouds need touching
up; the shadows beneath the bulges
look gray. Could he reach that far?
I'd hold the ladder.

His arm would stretch across the sky
and with a dash or two of light
he'd smooth away the shady parts,
and fill the cracks with gleaming white.

CHRISTINE E. HEMP

o o o

When I asked a class of fourth graders what I should write for this book, they said, "Write how you made the poem"; one student said, "Write a mystery story!" Though we laughed about the second idea, I later realized that, strangely, poem making and mystery go hand in hand.

I started "White on White" with no inkling the poem would end with my father painting the sky. The first line came while I sat on a lawn chair in June, a week before my sister's outdoor wedding. The *slap slap* of my father's paintbrush roused me to run get my yellow pad and pen (I like the colored fine-tips best). I love rhythms, so this poem at first seemed to be about the music of the brushstrokes: "Today my father is painting. . . ."

And then the mystery began. After I'd set the scene, words I didn't expect grew on the page: My father started painting our

81

cat Zooey and the flowers! He reached higher than the porch steps, the windows—or even the flagpole! I just let him do what he wanted in the poem. (After all, fathers can do most anything, can't they?)

To me, poetry is a marriage of craft and imagination. The making of a poem requires attention to form, sound, revision, and precision. (I must have revised at least ten drafts of this poem.) But imagination lifts you from a lawn chair to the clouds. And this is the mystery of poetry.

C. E. H.

• • •

Spring Thaw

MARK VINZ

Up and down March streets
small boys with basketballs
beneath torn nets or none at all
and Mother calling supper

just beyond the porch door's slap
the thudding ball is mud-caked
soaked from puddles, fingers numb
with only time for one last jump

shot, snowflakes fluttering
between the streetlights blinking
time for one more shot one
last time Mother calling more!

Black Hair

GARY SOTO

At eight I was brilliant with my body.
In July, that ring of heat
We all jumped through, I sat in the bleachers
Of Romain Playground, in the lengthening
Shade that rose from our dirty feet.

The game before us was more than baseball.
It was a figure—Hector Moreno,
Quick and hard with turned muscles,
His crouch the one I assumed before an altar
Of worn baseball cards, in my room.

I came here because I was Mexican, a stick
Of light in love with those
Who could do it—the triple and hard slide,
The gloves eating balls into double plays.
What could I do with 50 pounds, my shyness,
My black torch of hair, about to go out?
Father was dead, his face no longer
Hanging over the table or our sleep,
And mother was the dream of mouths
Twisting hurt by butter knives.

In the bleachers I was brilliant with my body,
Waving players in and stomping my feet,
Growing sweaty in the presence of white shirts.
I chewed sunflower seeds. I drank water
And bit my arm through the late innings.
When Hector lined balls in deep
Center, in my mind I rounded the bases
With him, my face flared, my hair lifting
Beautifully, because we were coming home
To the arms of brown people.

GARY SOTO

o   o   o

I was no good at baseball. For three springs I tried out for Little League, and each spring I waited by the telephone, praying that a coach would call me. He never did. I did, however, play pickup games at the playground, and although I was a poor fielder and too weak to hit to the outfield, I did manage to get on bases now and then. And once on base, I could run. I was fast and sneaky and game enough to steal bases.

My poem "Black Hair" is about watching others play baseball and is a poem of admiration for one person who could play extremely well. He was Mexican, like me, but unlike me he was "quick and hard with turned muscles," a great fielder, a strong hitter, and a leader whose presence you could feel in the dugout. He was beautiful to watch when he went down on a knee to pick up a grounder, and inspiring when he sent a ball flying over the head of the center fielder. He was Mexican and was better than anyone else. After hitting a home run, he and I became one—metaphorically, I mean—as we rounded the bases together. He made me feel pride.

G. S.

Baseball Cards #1

JIM DANIELS

One
of the 10,342 baseball cards in my parents' attic
sneezes in the darkness, remembers
sweaty hands.

He calls to me across hundreds of miles:
Remember me, Jake Wood, 1964, 2nd base,
    Detroit Tigers,
Series 2, No. 272?
He wants to stretch his legs, climb out
from between Wilbur Wood and the 4th Series
    Checklist
wants to outsail all the other cards
in a game of farthies, float down
on Jose Tartabull in a game of tops.
He wants to smell like fresh from the pack
wants to be perfumed again
with the pink smell of bubble gum.

October Saturday

BOBBI KATZ

All the leaves have turned to cornflakes.
It looks as if some giant's baby brother
had tipped the box
and scattered them upon our lawn—
millions and millions of cornflakes—
crunching, crunching under our feet.
When the wind blows,
they rattle against each other,
nervously chattering.

We rake them into piles—
Dad and I.
Piles and piles of cornflakes!
A breakfast for a whole family of giants!
We do not talk much as we rake—
a word here—
a word there.
The leaves are never silent.

Inside the house my mother is packing
short sleeved shirts and faded bathing suits—
rubber clogs and flippers—
in a box marked SUMMER.

We are raking,
Dad and I.

Raking, raking.
The sky is blue, then orange, then gray.
My arms are tired.
I am dreaming of the box marked SUMMER.

Bingo

PAUL B. JANECZKO

Saturday night
Dad washed, I dried
the supper dishes
while Mom armed herself
for Early Bird bingo at seven
in the church basement:
her lucky piece
(a smooth quarter she'd won the first time out),
seat cushion,
and a White Owls box of pink plastic markers.

Dad read the paper
watched TV with me
until Mom returned,
announcing her triumph with a door slam
and a shout
"I was hot!"

Flinging her hat,
twirling out of her jacket,
she pulled dollar bills
from her pockets
before setting them free
to flutter like fat spring snow.

"Ninety-two dollars!" she squealed
as Dad hugged her off the floor.
"Ninety-two dollars!"

In bed I listened to
mumbled voices
planning to spend the money—
on groceries
school clothes
a leaky radiator—
and wished she'd buy
a shiny red dress
long white gloves
and clickety-click high heels.

PAUL B. JANECZKO

o   o   o

Nothing in "Bingo" really happened to me, although the poem is based on my experiences. That may sound like a contradiction, but many poems are born of contradictions. Let me explain.

First, what didn't happen. (1) My mother never played bingo. (2) My father didn't wash the supper dishes before sitting down to enjoy the newspaper.

Now, the facts. (1) When I was in ninth grade I worked at the Monday night bingo games in our church basement. I remember the smoke, the buzz of conversations, and the periodic shrill shouts of "Bingo!" I recall the good luck charms and small statues of saints some of the bingo freaks brought to watch over them. (2) My father worked a second job repairing televisions and radios. On some nights he packed up his tool kit and drove off on a service call in our '56 Ford station wagon. On other nights he worked on a set in his workshop, a maze of wires, dials, and test equipment right out of a cheap science-fiction movie.

Many years later I realized that my mother didn't play bingo because there were kids at home who needed attention, clothes that needed to be washed or mended, homework that needed to be checked. My father didn't have much time to relax after supper with the newspaper because of his second job.

From this realization came "Bingo," which I consider to be a love poem. It's about parents loving their son and wanting their home to be a good place for him; the son loving his parents and wanting his mother to do something frivolous for herself with her winnings; and everyone wanting the best for the people they love.

P. B. J.

PART III

The Horses

MAXINE KUMIN

It has turned to snow in the night.
The horses have put on
their long fur stockings
and they are wearing
fur caps with high necks
out of which the device
of their ears makes four statues.
Their tails have caught flecks
of snow and hang down
loose as bedsheets.
They stand nose to nose
in the blue light that coats
the field before sunup
and rub dry their old kisses.

• • •

How Birds Should Die

PAUL ZIMMER

Not like hailstones
ricocheting off concrete
nor vaporized through
jets nor drubbed
against windshields
not in flocks
plunged down into
cold sea by
sudden weather no
please no but
like stricken cherubim
spreading on winds
their tiny engines
suddenly taken out
by small pains
they sigh and
float down on
sunlit updrafts
drifting through treetops
to tumble gently
onto the moss

The Sea Gull's Eye

RUSSELL HOBAN

The thing about a gull is not the soaring flight,
    the creaking cry;
The thing about a sea gull is its eye—
Eye of the wind, the ocean's eye, not pretty,
Black at the center of its yellow stare, no pity
And no fear in it, nor reason, nothing warm
To shelter its own wildness from the storm—
Naked life only, disdainful of its form.

Along the harbor road the other day
I found a broken sea gull where it lay
Great-winged and skyless, wrecked by stone or shot—
Some boy, perhaps, had done it who had not
More pity than his prey
And there it lay
And lived awhile, until that yellow eye
No longer looked out on the ocean sky,
And life, indifferent to boys with stones,
Flew up again with crows that picked the bones.

Photo by Tana Hoban

RUSSELL HOBAN

o   o   o

Poetry is something I've felt differently about at different times in my life. There have been times when I've read poetry almost every day and times when I haven't read it for years.

My feelings about poets change, too. For a long time I didn't know I cared all that much about Auden until I noticed all the paper markers sticking out of the book. I'm not sure how much I like Eliot but my forty-five-year-old copy of *Four Quartets* is almost falling apart from use, and if the house were on fire that would be one of the books I'd grab. If I could have the work of just one poet on a desert island I think it might be Rilke, provided my wife were shipwrecked with me to translate the poems (the published translations always attempt to be literary and are never accurate). Rilke's thoughts are thoughts you can go on thinking about for a long time. For example, from the "First Duino Elegy":

> *Denn das Schöne ist nichts*
> For Beauty is nothing
> *als des Schrecklichen Anfang, . . .*
> but the beginning of Terror, . . .

and further along in the same poem:

> *. . . und die findigen Tiere merken es schon,*
> . . . and the shrewd animals have already noticed
> *dass wir nicht sehr verlässlich zu Haus sind*
> that we are not very reliably at home
> *in der gedeuteten Welt . . .*
> in the interpreted world . . .

What we call reality is after all only an interpretation of the world and it never quite works, never quite accounts for everything. Poetry, questing always on that shifting edge between beauty and terror, finds the missing words that fill in the picture and make us a little more at home in the world.

R. H.

The Passenger Pigeon

PAUL FLEISCHMAN

We were counted not in	
	thousands
nor	
	millions
but in	
billions.	*billions.*
	We were numerous as the
stars	stars
	in the heavens
As grains of	
sand	sand
at the sea	
	As the
buffalo	buffalo
	on the plains.
When we burst into flight	
	we so filled the sky

that the
sun   sun
was darkened
                                 and
day   day
                                 became dusk.
Humblers of the sun   Humblers of the sun
we were!   we were!
The world
inconceivable   inconceivable
                                without us.

Yet it's 1914,
and here I am
alone   alone
                                caged in the Cincinnati Zoo.

the last

                                of the passenger pigeons.

PAUL FLEISCHMAN

o o o

"Poetry begins in the mouth," the poet Donald Hall has written. For me, it began as well with the shortwave radio, the alto recorder, and the Swiss Army knife.

I received the radio when I was ten. After my parents and sisters had gone to bed, I would plug in the headphones and cruise the airwaves, no light in the room but the radio's dials. I heard broadcasts in Japanese, Swedish, Arabic, Hindi, and dozens of other languages I didn't speak. Not knowing the sense of the words, I heard only their sound—their music.

I learned to play the recorder in high school. A few years later I became friends with a flute player. For hours on end we played duets, never wanting to stop. I discovered that two voices were much better than one. And that performing a piece was infinitely more fun than merely listening to it.

The knife was a twenty-first birthday present. Since childhood I'd made impromptu sculptures out of driftwood, pine needles—whatever was at hand. But that knife had an awl, perfect for making holes. A technological leap that spurred a burst of building that still hasn't subsided.

In consequence of all of which, I was struck one day by the desire to write some poems for two voices. Verbal music, making use of the sounds of words as much as their meaning. Duets for two readers, to be performed aloud. Sculptures built not of sticks, but words. I've never enjoyed writing anything else as much.

P. F.

JOANNE RYDER

Like magic,
thin green sticks
rise from the weeds
soar over the water
and stop,
hanging in
sunny space.
You wonder how
the trick is done
until you see
long wings
clear as glass.
And if you had
one wish today,
you'd ask for
dragonfly wings
in just your size
to surprise
to surprise.

Photo by Deborah Yaffe

JOANNE RYDER

o o o

When I was young I liked to read fantasy stories about magical creatures and far distant worlds. I thought when I grew up I would write stories like those. But I discovered writing poetry; and now my poems are filled with people and animals and the magic I see in the real world around me. I don't go to faraway lands to find and imagine wonderful things—a handful of treasure, invisible wings, boxes hiding secrets in the woods. Amazing things are all around me, appearing ordinary at first, until I really look at them closely.

As I write about them, the real things become very new, more vivid and full of color. That's exciting to me, and I look at my own world through a new window, my poem, and see the marvels all around.

J. R.

Spruce Woods

A. R. AMMONS

It's so still
today that a
dipping bough means
a squirrel
has gone through.

A. R. AMMONS

o   o   o

We study each other from the earliest age to see how to behave. Much of our behavior may be born with us, but a fine-tuning, at least, has to take place before we fit like natives in a group. One place to watch behavior is in poems, not just what they say, but how they say it. Do poems sound like loudmouths, or do they whisper their best stuff? Do they warp our feelings to win arguments unfairly, or are they open, honest, thoughtful? Do they please us with sweet talk, or do they speak sincerely with a few words? Does the poem stand for formal behavior, as for a wedding, or very casual ways, as for a picnic? The ways poems come on to us give us something to think about and choose between, something to be like or not, something to fight for or forget about. Poems are like people and sometimes mean the opposite of what they say. But from the behavior of poems and people, we learn a little better to know how we feel and to say what we mean.

A. R. A.

Mike and Major

CYNTHIA RYLANT

Mike's sister said he
listened to Lawrence Welk records
and cried.
But it didn't matter to me.
Mike rode a 10-speed bike
when they were still called
English.
And he had a collie dog
named Major.
Major so majestic
trotting beside that
English bicycle.
Understanding Beaver
better than us all.
Mike loved The Beatles, too.
So we listened together,
us three.
Major finally grew old
and one day didn't see
a car
Mike all alone on his bike.
Carrying that pain
until
he could
drive.

CYNTHIA RYLANT

o o o

I was afraid of writing poetry for the longest time because I wasn't any good at rhyming, and I thought poetry had to be complicated and very, very deep. I didn't know that the very way I *looked* at things was poetry. I mean, I notice things other people don't and usually it has something to do with the way one small thing means so much. I once met a boy who had read my book of poems about growing up in Beaver, West Virginia (*Waiting to Waltz ... A Childhood*) and he said to me, "I know just what you mean about Todd's Hardware Store. Every time I walk into the Western Auto Store in this little town I live in ..." And he proceeded to describe to me what it was about the Western Auto Store that hit him the way a good sunset hits you and I thought to myself, This boy's a poet. I believe he was born with that way of looking at things, as I was, and even if he never writes one single line of poetry, he'll always *be* a poet. And the people around him will mutter about how intense he can get sometimes and his teachers will complain about how he never pays enough attention and people will wonder why he can't just *lighten up* and watch "The Cosby Show" with them. What they don't understand is that he's seeing all those small, meaningful things they're missing, and it sucks away so much of your soul and energy when you're trying to make sense of what you see with your poet's heart. They will want him to be a regular Joe and he will *never* be able to be that, and because of it he will feel lonelier than most people—even though he may be a popular boy—and he will wonder why he can't live a normal life like everybody else. He will wonder why he hurts so much sometimes. Why he feels so *different* from everybody else who's just fitting right in to all the systems: everybody else who's getting the gold stars at school, or marrying and settling into a nice job in a nice town and finding a nice wife and having four nice kids and keeping a nice lawn and a nice clean car. He will too often feel like a failure, and he will too often never pick up a pen and try to get published because he doesn't know what a good poet he is since there's no test that told him so. A lot of people think they can write poetry, and many do, because they can figure out how to line up the words, or make certain sounds rhyme, or just imitate the other poets they've read. But this boy, *he's* the real poet, because when he tries to put on paper what he's seen with his heart, he will believe deep down there are no good words for it, no words can do it, and at that moment he will have begun to write poetry.

C. R.

dog

VALERIE WORTH

Under a maple tree
The dog lies down,
Lolls his limp
Tongue, yawns,
Rests his long chin
Carefully between
Front paws;
Looks up, alert;
Chops, with heavy
Jaws, at a slow fly,
Blinks, rolls
On his side,
Sighs, closes
His eyes: sleeps
All afternoon
In his loose skin.

Po's Garden

REE YOUNG

In Grandmother's
larkspur garden, a cat
sleeps, his one blue eye
hidden by a yellow-furred
lid. His dark nose
twitches, flares, scans
the air for a scent
familiar and friendly.
He knows me, this cat
with glossy gold coat,
waits for me, stretching
like a breeze blown
down the hillside, slow
and long. We lounge
all day in the garden's
shade and count
butterflies.

REE YOUNG

o o o

"How do you start being a poet?" Jesse, my ten-year-old son, asked me.

I had to pause and think hard because I wasn't really sure. Then I told him the way I knew best—how I started.

"One day I found there was something I wanted to tell someone else . . . I don't recall what it was, something happy or painful or funny. But the word patterns I usually used didn't seem to express what I wanted to say. So, I wrote it down, and instead of a letter, the thought came out as a poem. It had a flow that other writing didn't have."

"I see," said Jesse. "It's not like talking or reading from a journal or newspaper. That's just blab—blab—blab. Poetry is like listening to water and wanting to write down what you hear."

R. Y.

Merry-Go-Round

PATRICIA HUBBELL

I rode a golden carousel
across a tattered town,
(with an up pony, up pony, up pony, down).
Far across the tattered town
the carousel sped—
(The carousel was living
and the town was dead.)
The faces of the people
swirled around,
blurred and blended
in calliope sound.
The golden ponies shivered
and my hand clutched mane,
The shrilling of calliope
filled my brain
with an up pony, up pony, up pony, down;
(around me pulsed the tatters
of the torn, dead town).
I was whirling carousel, carousel was me,
We were the living,
wild and free.

PATRICIA HUBBELL

o   o   o

When I was ten years old, I started a museum in the playhouse in our backyard. I filled the shelves with birds' nests, rocks, shells, pressed wildflowers, and other treasures. I spent hours in the woods and fields collecting things. I took long walks and kept my eyes eagerly open.

One day, I found a snakeskin, complete from head to tail. The thin, papery skin was beautiful. I put it on a shelf where the sun would shine through it.

About the time I started the museum, I began to write poems. I wrote about the sun and the rain, about riding my pony, about swimming in the ocean. I wrote about the things in my museum. Birds' nests and rocks, leaves and butterflies found their way into the poems.

115

I think, in a way, a poem is like a museum. It's a place where you can keep safe the things you love or that you find interesting. You can keep a beautiful snakeskin in a poem, and you can keep the look of the sun shining through it. You can keep the papery feel, and the rustle the skin makes when you pick it up. You can keep the excitement.

In a poem, you can keep things you could never put in a real museum—things like a ride on a merry-go-round. You can keep feelings of sadness and joy. You can keep love, safe forever.

P. H.

When It Is Snowing

SIV CEDERING

When it is snowing
the blue jay
is the only piece of
sky
in my
backyard.

SIV CEDERING

o   o   o

One day when it was snowing, I noticed how colorless every-thing looked outside. The snow on the ground, on the rooftops, and on the branches was a dull white, the sky was grayish white, even the evergreens were more gray than green. Then suddenly I saw a blue jay in a tree. The bright blue of its feathers reminded me of how surprisingly blue the sky looks when it clears after a snowstorm. That in turn reminded me of how the snow glitters when the sun comes out, and how that brilliant snow shows off the deep greens of evergreens, the bright red of barns, or the rusty red of brick buildings. Like that blue bird, a poem is often small, but it can surprise you. With words it can paint a picture that in turn leads to other pictures and thoughts. So when you see a poem, read it as carefully as you would open a surprise package. And someday when it is snowing, or some night when everyone is asleep, try writing a little poem.

S. C.

• • •

Icebox

JOHN UPDIKE

In Daddy's day there were such things:
   Wood cabinets of cool
In which a cake of ice was placed
   While he was off at school.

Blue-veined, partitioned in itself,
   The cake seemed cut of air
Which had exploded; one cracked star
   Appeared imprisoned there.

It melted slowly through the day;
   The metal slats beneath
Seeped upwards, so the slippery base
   Developed downward teeth.

Eventually an egg so small
   It could be tossed away,
The ice cake vanished quite, as has
   That rather distant day.

JOHN UPDIKE

o   o   o

These stanzas were part of *A Cheerful Alphabet of Pleasant Objects*, from Apple to Zeppelin, written in 1957 and dedicated to my son, who was then less than one year old. That is why I speak of "Daddy's day" in the first line. Iceboxes were very common when I was a little boy, in the 1930s; they preceded refrigerators in the American kitchen. Instead of an electric engine to produce coldness, though, the icebox simply had a large cake of ice in it, perhaps a foot square, which was brought every other day or so by an "iceman" in his "ice truck." The ice was manufactured, by electrical cooling, in an "ice plant." As a child I lived near an ice plant and used to watch the men handle the big slabs of ice with big tongs and break them into smaller pieces with "ice picks." Every kitchen used to have in one of its drawers an ice pick, to break smaller pieces off of the ice in the icebox. The ice plant supplied each home with a card you could put in the window, saying if you wanted ice that day, and how big a piece.

What I explain here in prose my poem tries to suggest with poetry. More, the poem tries to convey the look of the cake, or block, of ice—how it had a kind of star in it, and how as it melted the slats it sat on would rise up inside it like teeth. Poetry tries to give the look and the feel of a thing or experience, in language that makes us stop and think, and that often tries to impress itself on our minds with rhyme and meter. The rhyme scheme here is *abcb*, and the lines are alternately iambic tetrameter and iambic trimeter: that is, they alternately have four beats and three, so that it's as if two seven-beat lines rhyme. When you write poetry, you hear this music in your head, like singing a song to yourself. It's not too hard, and it's fun.

J. U.

Haunted House

VALERIE WORTH

Its echoes,
Its aching stairs,
Its doors gone stiff
At the hinges,

Remind us of its
Owners, who
Grew old, who
Died, but

Who are still
Here: leaning
In the closet like
That curtain rod,

Sleeping on the cellar
Shelf like this
Empty
Jelly jar.

VALERIE WORTH

o   o   o

Some of the subjects I write about in my poetry might seem ordinary or trivial—but to me they have fascinating qualities that go beyond their simple appearance.

One of poetry's most wonderful features is that it can get beneath the surface of things and explore them not as mere objects but as remarkable phenomena with lively personalities of their own. Even such common articles as coat hangers can take on unexpected dimensions within the realm of a poem; and if this can happen with coat hangers, then the world must be filled with other "ordinary" subjects just waiting for poetry to come along and reveal their extraordinary selves.

This is certainly how I see them; and it is why I write about them the way I do.

V. W.

A Hardware Store As Proof of the Existence of God

NANCY WILLARD

I praise the brightness of hammers pointing east
like the steel woodpeckers of the future,
and dozens of hinges opening brass wings,
and six new rakes shyly fanning their toes,
and bins of hooks glittering into bees,

And a rack of wrenches like the long bones of
    horses,
and mailboxes sowing rows of silver chapels,
and a company of plungers waiting for God
to claim their thin legs in their big shoes
and put them on and walk away laughing.

In a world not perfect but not bad either
let there be glue, glaze, gum, and grabs,
caulk also, and hooks, shackles, cables, and slips,
and signs so spare a child may read them,
Men, Women, In, Out, No Parking, Beware the Dog.

In the right hands, they can work wonders.

Watering Trough

MAXINE KUMIN

Let the end of all bathtubs
be this putting out to pasture
of four Victorian bowlegs
anchored in grasses.

Let all longnecked browsers
come drink from the shallows
while faucets grow rusty
and porcelain yellows.

Where once our nude forebears
soaped up in this vessel
come, cows, and come, horses.
Bring burdock and thistle,

come slaver the scum of
timothy and clover
on the castiron lip that
our grandsires climbed over

and let there be always
green water for sipping
that muzzles may enter thoughtful
and rise dripping.

MAXINE KUMIN

o o o

My life as a poet! Sometimes it is hard to believe I am a poet. We live on an old farm in central New Hampshire, and we breed and raise horses for distance riding. We also have a few sheep, two dogs, two cats, a serious vegetable garden, and a sugar bush, which is what country people call a stand of maple trees to tap for syrup. We set a hundred taps every March. All summer long we work in the garden; I freeze, can, make jams and pickles. And 365 days of the year the animals must be fed and watered, exercised and schooled, and so on.

But this is where my poems come from. Often I don't know a poem is starting until long after the event that gave rise to it. The idea has to form slowly. Then it sort of knocks and asks for attention. Over the years I have learned to pay attention to these glimmers of beginnings. I try to write in the mornings, after the barn chores are finished, and before much else is happening. I am a morning person, so I think I have more brain cells at 6 A.M. than at 6 P.M.

A poem is portable. You can carry it around with you in your head for days while you work on it in secret. Most of my poems go through several drafts on paper, and not every idea for a poem works out. I have a big cardboard box full of scraps and snippets that never quite turned into poems. I don't throw these out because sometimes one will jump out of the pile and begin a whole new poem, one I hadn't thought about at all. Poetry is full of surprises. I think I'm especially lucky as a poet because my two worlds overlap.

M. K.

Deserted Farm

MARK VINZ

Where the barn stood
the empty milking stalls rise up
like the skeleton of an ancient sea beast,
exiled forever on shores of prairie.

Decaying timber moans softly in twilight:
the house collapses like a broken prayer.
Tomorrow the heavy lilac blossoms will open,
higher than the roofbeams, reeling in wind.

MARK VINZ

o   o   o

I think the reason I first learned to love poems as a small child was because they allowed me to see things in a very different way from the ordinary, and to this day my definition of what a poem is comes down to this special kind of seeing. One of the poems I remember my mother reading to me when I was three or four years old was called "The Moon Is the North Wind's Cookie." How I loved to imagine those images, flying off to wherever a poem could take me in my imagination. But as I grew older I learned to value the ways poems taught me to look at real, everyday things, too. What I had learned is that poems have many different ways of helping us to see.

What we have to remember, I think, is that poems come from many, many different places—from dreams and fantasies, to be sure, but also from everything else that goes on inside and all around us. That's how poems teach us to see, over and over again—through their special and surprising use of words, and through encouraging us to feel, to think, and to use our imaginations. I don't know of anything else that can offer us so much.

M. V.

PART IV

The Poem That Got Away

FELICE HOLMAN

There I was and in it came
Through the fogbank of my brain
From the fastness of my soul
Shining like a glowing coal—
The nearly perfect poem!

Oh, it may have needed just
An alteration here or there—
A little tuck, a little seam
to be exactly what I mean—
The really perfect poem.

I'll write it later on, I said,
The idea's clear and so's my head.
This pen I have is nearly dry.
What I'll do now is finish this pie,
Then on to the perfect poem!

With pen in hand quite full of ink
I try now to recall.
I've plenty of time in which to think
But the poem went down the kitchen sink
With the last of the perfect pie.

CHARLOTTE POMERANTZ

Roses and a tulip
and a ripe green pear.
All are on the table
by my rocking chair.
When you come to visit,
you will see them there;
unless, of course, I've eaten up
the ripe green pear.

CHARLOTTE POMERANTZ

If anyone were to pose to me the classic question, What one book would you take to a desert island? I would answer, a big, unabridged English dictionary. (This assumes, of course, that the desert island has electricity and running water. Otherwise, I'd exchange the dictionary for a "how-to" book.)

I think I could live happily among all those words until company arrived.

C. P.

KARLA KUSKIN

Write about a radish
Too many people write about the moon.

The night is black
The stars are small and high
The clock unwinds its ever-ticking tune
Hills gleam dimly
Distant nighthawks cry.
A radish rises in the waiting sky.

KARLA KUSKIN

o o o

When I used to carry a camera with me and take a lot of photographs, I paid very close attention to everything I saw. And I noticed that when I had color film in my camera my eye would be especially aware of colorful scenery, or people dressed in interesting color combinations.

But when my camera was loaded with black-and-white film I paid much more attention to light and dark, overall pattern and design, the kind of things that would show up well in black-and-white photographs. There is also a difference in my point of view when I am writing prose and when I am writing poetry.

Writing prose makes me listen for stories. But if I am writing poetry I concentrate more on the rhythms and sounds of words, and on details. The smallest observation can be the start of a poem. I thought of "I have a friend ..." as I tried to talk to my daughter Julia (then about seven years old) while she endlessly practiced standing on her hands. And "Write about a radish" began as advice to myself on a day when I was determined to write a poem about something nobody else had ever written a poem about.

So that I will not forget a particular combination of words or a funny idea I make notes. If a notebook is not handy I will use any scrap of paper lying around: my grocery list, the edge of the newspaper. You cannot only write a poem *about* anything, you can also write it *on* almost anything. Poems also make nice gifts and they never need to be walked or fed.

K. K.

Poem

ROBERT CURRIE

If
I write
a

n
a
r
r
o
w

poem
lean
as a
famine
someday
I'll find
an editor
with
a space
about
-this wide-
then
you
fat guys
can sweat
in the
steam baths
while
I
move
in

ROBERT CURRIE

o   o   o

Almost every poet has his own unique idea of what poetry
is. Dylan Thomas, for example, said, "Poetry is what makes my
toenails twinkle." Well, true poetry is complex enough to en-
compass even the wildest definitions. I like to think of poetry
as a heightened response to life, experience closely observed
or highly imagined, then touched somehow by an indefinable
magic as it's preserved on paper. One of the key words here
is "somehow," for in many ways poetry is beyond explanation,
simply because its source is so often in the subconscious. Another
key word is "magic." I think the best poems are marked by
magic; they grow through a kind of wizardry which even the
greatest poets cannot completely understand, let alone explain.

I'm not talking about the mere tricks of a magician here. This is real sorcery. There's an element of miracle involved. The poet imagines a specific situation, perhaps a real one, and asks himself, "What if?" What if this could happen—or this? And then it happens, because the poet lets the magic flow, allowing the poem to develop as it must, carrying him where it will.

Of course, the poet must exercise his craftsmanship to make the poem as good as it can be. He must select the concrete details, the vivid images that allow his poem to live. He must search for the form from which the poem can grow most naturally, for the sounds and rhythms which best emphasize what he has to say. Above all, he must struggle for the best possible words and get them in the best possible order. In short, he must polish the poem until it shines. In the end, if he's lucky, it may even make his toenails twinkle.

R. C.

Thoughts That Were Put into Words

KARLA KUSKIN

Thoughts that were put into words
Have been said.
The words were then spoken
And written
And read.
Take a look and go on
We are practically done.

The leftover afternoon light
Slips away
On a wind like a sigh.
Watch the day curtains close,
Hear the wind going grey
At the edge of the edge
You and I
Turn the page
Read its message
"The End."

Does the end mean good-bye?

Burning Bright

LILLIAN MORRISON

A mermaid's tears
have silver fish in them,
a tiger's,
yellow stars.
Mine have spikes
and spokes of bikes
and yours
have blue guitars.

• • •

Valentine for Ernest Mann

NAOMI SHIHAB NYE

You can't order a poem like you order a taco.
Walk up to the counter, say, "I'll take two"
and expect it to be handed back to you
on a shiny plate.

Still, I like your spirit.
Anyone who says, "Here's my address,
write me a poem," deserves something in reply.
So I'll tell you a secret instead:
poems hide. In the bottoms of our shoes,
they are sleeping. They are the shadows
drifting across our ceilings the moment
before we wake up. What we have to do
is live in a way that lets us find them.

Once I knew a man who gave his wife
two skunks for a valentine.
He couldn't understand why she was crying.
"I thought they had such beautiful eyes."

And he was serious. He was a serious man
who lived in a serious way. Nothing was ugly
just because the world said so. He really
liked those skunks. So, he re-invented them
as valentines and they became beautiful.
At least, to him. And the poems that had been
   hiding
in the eyes of skunks for centuries
crawled out and curled up at his feet.

Maybe if we re-invent whatever our lives give us,
we find poems. Check your garage, the odd sock
in your drawer, the person you almost like, but
   not quite.

And let me know.

ACKNOWLEDGMENTS

Permission to reprint copyrighted poems is gratefully acknowledged to the following:

Another Chicago Press, for "What I Remember About the 6th Grade" by Mark Vinz, Copyright © 1987 by Mark Vinz (first appeared in *Another Chicago Magazine*, No. 17).

Atheneum Publishers, an imprint of Macmillan Publishing Company, for "Merry-Go-Round" by Patricia Hubbell from *Catch Me a Wind*, Copyright © 1968 by Patricia Hubbell. Comment on "Merry-Go-Round" Copyright © 1990 by Patricia Hubbell.

Bradbury Press, an affiliate of Macmillan, Inc., for "Pet Rock" and "Forgotten" and "Mike and Major" by Cynthia Rylant from *Waiting to Waltz* by Cynthia Rylant, Copyright © 1984 by Cynthia Rylant. Comment on "Mike and Major" Copyright © 1990 by Cynthia Rylant.

Breitenbush Books, Inc., for "Famous" by Naomi Shihab Nye from *Hugging the Jukebox* by Naomi Shihab Nye, Copyright © 1982 by Naomi Shihab Nye.

Gwendolyn Brooks, for "A Little Girl's Poem" and "Computer" from *Very Young Poets*, Copyright © 1983 by The David Company, Chicago. Comment on "A Little Girl's Room" and "Computer" Copyright © 1990 by Gwendolyn Brooks.

Curtis Brown, Ltd., for "The Horses" by Maxine Kumin from *Up Country* by Maxine Kumin, Copyright © 1972 by Maxine Kumin.

Siv Cedering, for "Suppose" from *Color Poems* published by Calliopea Press, Copyright © 1978 by Siv Cedering and "When It Is Snowing" from *The Juggler* published by Sagarin Press, Copyright © 1977 by Siv Cedering. Comment on "When It Is Snowing" Copyright © 1990 by Siv Cedering.

William Cole, for "The Panteater," Copyright © 1978 by William Cole. Comment on "The Panteater" Copyright © 1990 by William Cole.

Julia Cunningham, for "A short long story" and "Carousel," Copyright © by Julia Cunningham. Comment on "Carousel" Copyright © 1990 by Julia Cunningham.

Robert Currie, for "Poem" from *Sawdust and Dirt* published by Fiddlehead Poetry Books, Copyright © 1973. Comment on "Poem" Copyright © 1990 by Robert Currie.

Jim Daniels, for "Baseball Cards #1" reprinted from *The Long Ball* by Jim Daniels by permission of Pig In A Poke Press, Copyright © 1988 by Jim Daniels and "Speech Class," reprinted by permission of the author Copy-

146

INDEX OF POETS